Meet
Woof & Quack

For new friends and true friends. —J.A.S.

To my love, Hiroko, who is an individual like Quack. —R.S.

Text copyright © 2017 by Jamie A. Swenson
Illustrations copyright © 2017 by Ryan Sias

First Green Light Readers edition 2017

For information about permission to reproduce selections from this book, write to trade.permissions@hmhco.com or to Permissions, Houghton Mifflin Harcourt Publishing Company, 3 Park Avenue, 19th Floor, New York, New York 10016.

www.hmhco.com

The text of this book is set in ITC Lubalin Graph Std.
The display type was set in ITC Lubalin Graph Std.

Library of Congress Cataloging-in-Publication Data is on file.

ISBN: 978-0-544-95951-4 paper over board
ISBN: 978-0-544-95928-6 paperback

Manufactured in China
SCP 10 9 8 7 6 5 4 3 2 1
4500661225

Meet
Woof & Quack

by Jamie A. Swenson

illustrated by Ryan Sias

Houghton Mifflin Harcourt
Boston   New York

Let's play Fetch.

Fetch?

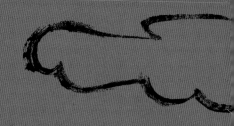

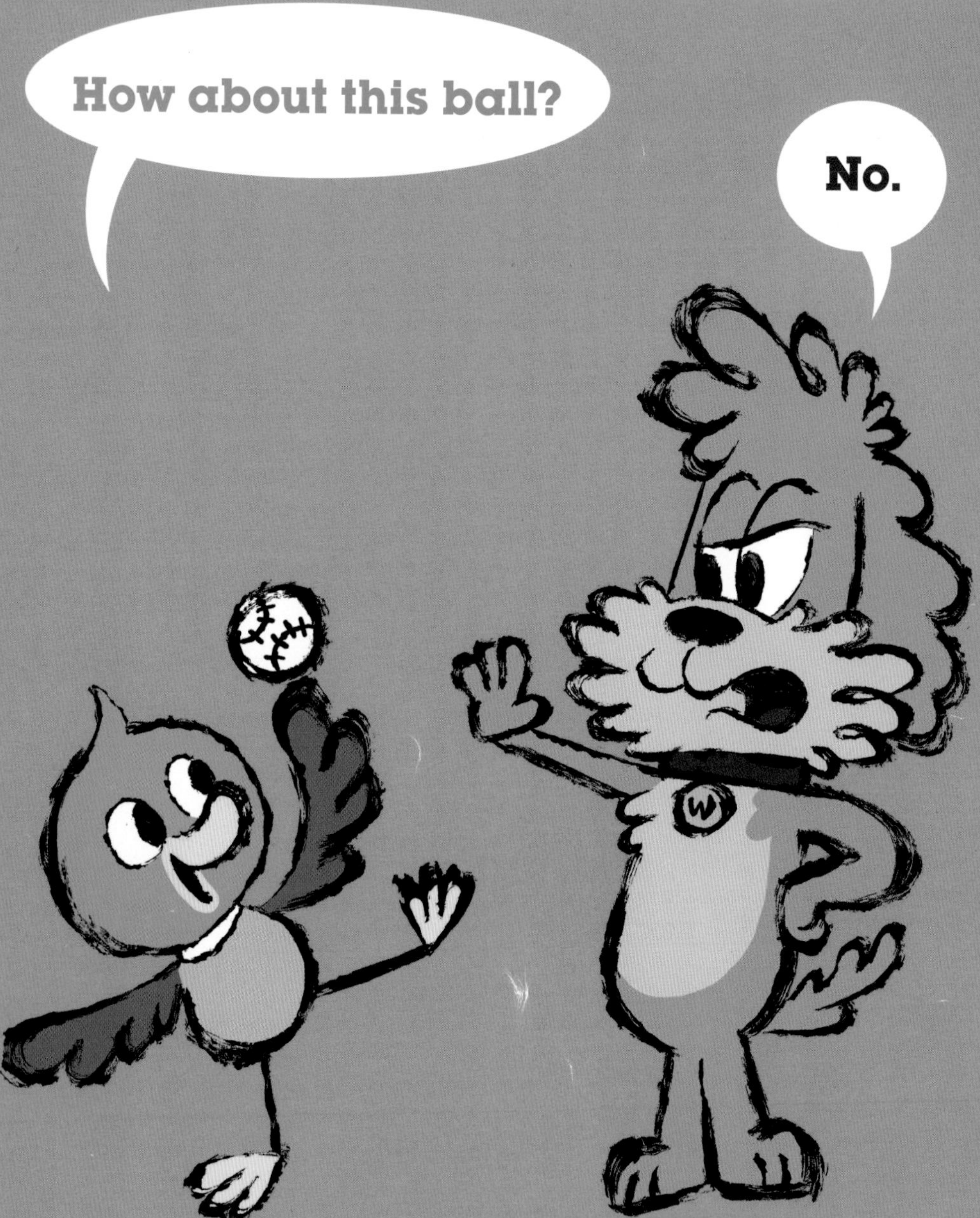
How about this ball?
No.

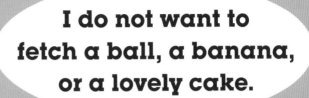

Woof threw the ball.

SWOOSH

Quack fetched the ball.

Woof threw the banana.

Quack fetched the banana.

Woof threw the lovely cake.

Do you like to eat cake?

I am a dog who loves to eat cake!

And I am a duck who loves to eat cake!

You are my kind of duck.

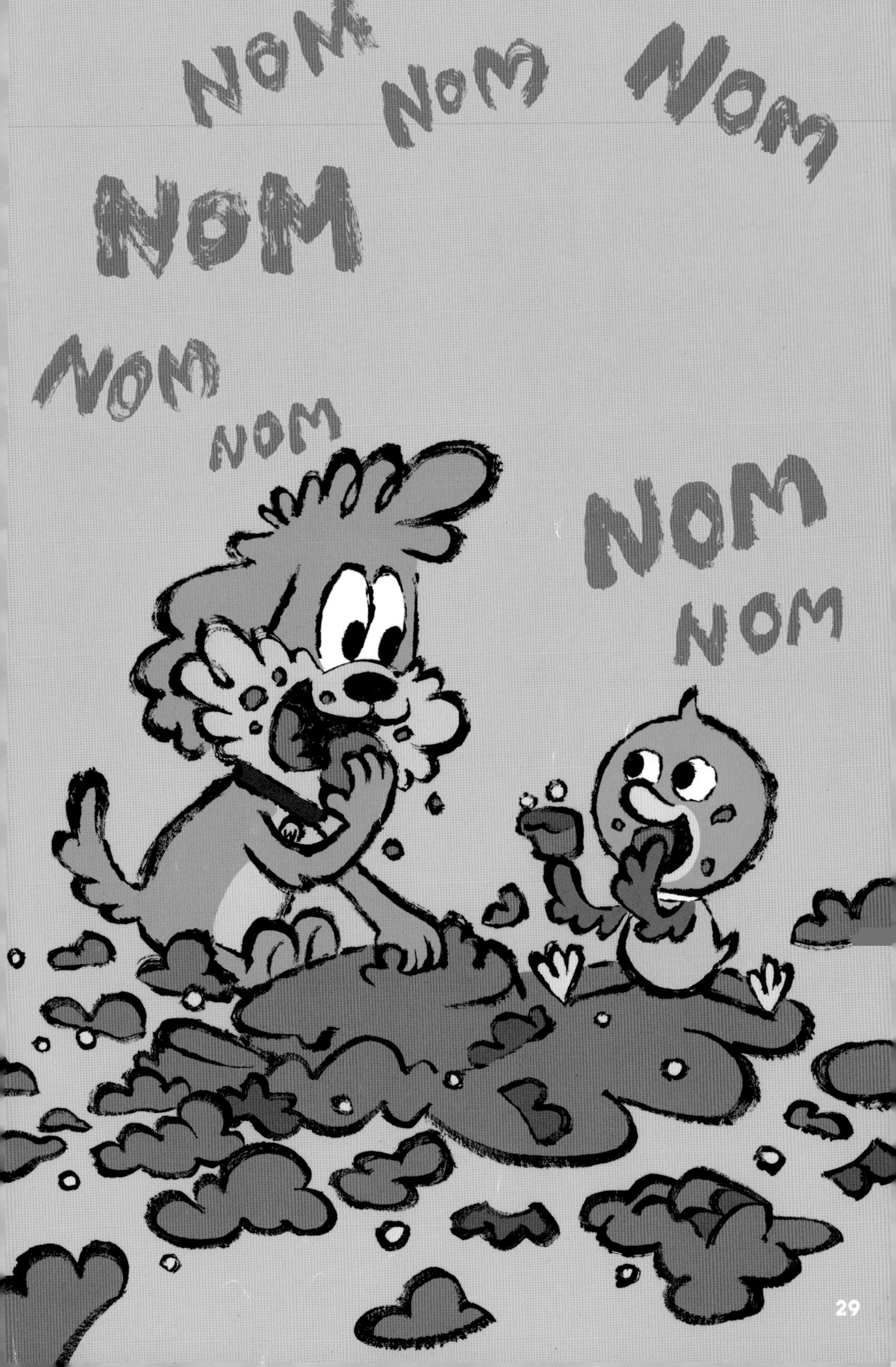
NOM
NOM
NOM
NOM
NOM
NOM
NOM
NOM